THE LION INSIDE

For River, whose teenifulness has already made our hearts hugesome. We love you so incredibly much - R. E.

For Lee Gleave, who left us too soon - J. F.

ORCHARD BOOKS
Carmelite House
50 Victoria Embankment
London EC4Y 0DZ

First published in 2015 by Orchard Books
This edition first published in 2016
ISBN 9 781 40833 1 606

Text © Rachel Bright 2015
Illustrations © Jim Field 2015

A CIP catalogue record for this book is available from the British Library.

12

Printed in China

Orchard Books
An imprint of Hachette Children's Group
Part of The Watts Publishing Group Limited
An Hachette UK Company
www.hachette.co.uk

FSC
www.fsc.org
MIX
Paper from
responsible sources
FSC® C104740

THE LiON INSIDE

Rachel Bright Jim Field

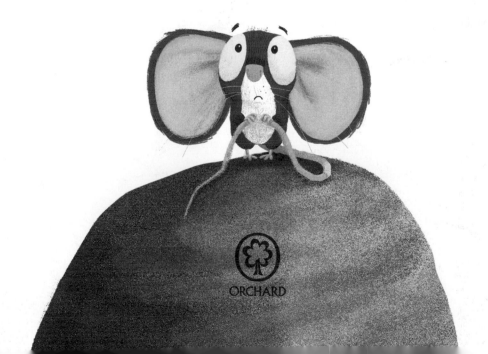

ORCHARD

In a dry dusty place where
the sand sparkled gold,
Stood a mighty flat rock —
all craggy and old.

And under that rock
in a tinyful house,
Lived the littlest, quietest,
meekest brown mouse.

He was so very tiny,
so incredibly small . . .
That nobody noticed him
EVER . . . at all.

He got trod on and sat on
and missed out for stuff.
Ignored and forgotten.

Yes . . .
mouse-life was tough.

Meanwhile, far above,
ON TOP of the rock,
Times were quite different.
It was **LION** o'clock!

This huge, toothsome creature
made sure EVERYONE saw
How IMPORTANT he was
by how loud he could . . .

He was **HEAD** of the pack.
He was **SHOUTY** and **TOUGH**.

He loved showing the crowd he was made of **STRONG STUFF**.

Yes, ALL were impressed
by this mighty King Cat.
"If only," thought Mouse,
"I could be more like that . . . ."

Then, late one dark night, in his mini-mouse bed,
the cleverest thought popped into his head.
He jumped from the covers and held up a paw.
"I've got it!" he said. "What I need is
a ROAR!"

"... I mean, what if this mouse
with the weeniest squeak
Was a little more GRRRRRRRR
and a little less meek?"

"Well, he'd still be
the smallest of fuzzy brown mice
but he'd make friends and join in.
And life would be nice."

"Yes!" thought the mouse.
"I **MUST** find out how!
I will learn how to roar and
I **WILL** learn it **NOW!**"

But —**GULP**— oh my gosh,
there was only **ONE** beast
who could teach him this thing
BUT might make him
. . . a **FEAST!**

It was time to be strong,
take a chance . . . after all,
Forever was such a long time
to feel small.

So he made himself brave
and he thought like a WINNER.
He set off for the top . . .
hoping not to be dinner!

It felt like the scariest thing
he could do . . .
But if you want things to change,
you first have to change **You**.

The further he climbed,
the closer he got
To the slumbering lion
reclining on top.

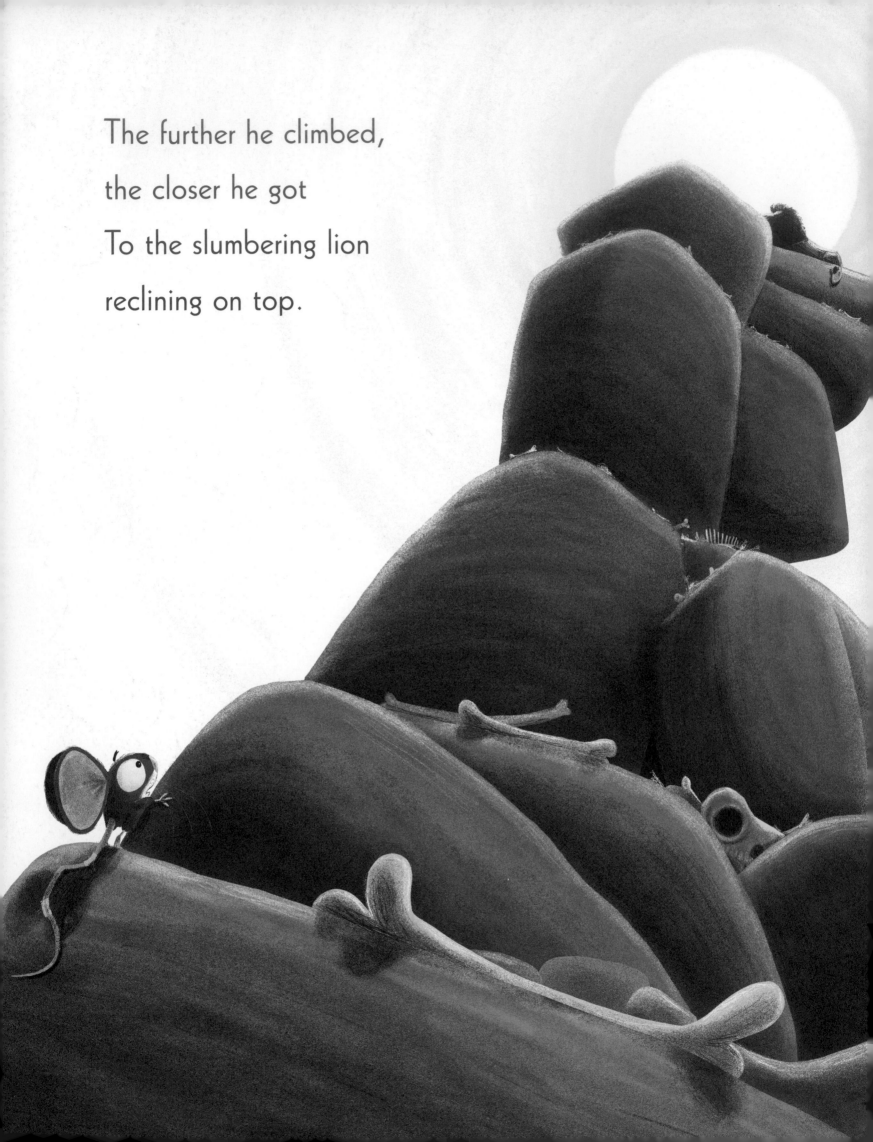

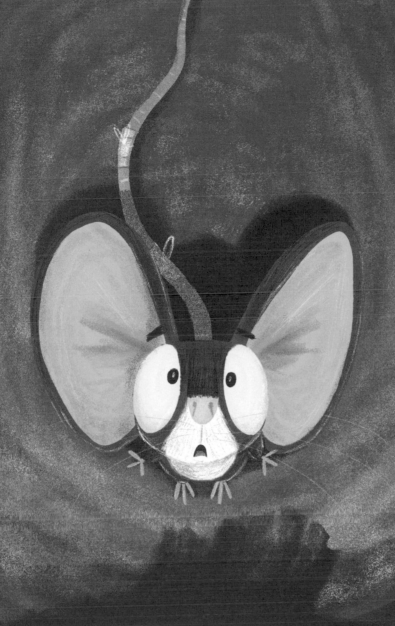

Then, at last, as he stood

on his tippity-toes,

He found himself

suddenly nose to . . .

. . . NOSE.

"Ahem, GULP, pardon me.

Wake up, Mr Lion, you've got company!

Um, SqUEAK, Mr Lion, what I've come to you for

Is SqUEAK . . . do you think you could teach

me your roar?"

A silence befell that twinkling plain.

Lion opened his eyes and puffed out his mane . . .

Time slowed right down — why, it felt like a week.

Then he opened his mouth . . . and let out an . . .

The lion was shaking. His paws all a-fumble.

He was backing away with a scrambling tumble.

"Don't hurt me," he whimpered. "Oh! Try to be nice."

Well, my goodness, this lion was frightened of mice!

"Don't worry," Mouse peeped.
"I'm a friend, not a foe.
Let's **ROCK** this together.
We'll have **FUN**, don't you know."

That was a magical moment for sure . . .
when mouse didn't feel AT ALL small any more.
He had found his true voice and learned to speak out,
and for THAT you don't need to roar or to shout.

And from that day and always, the two were a pair.

They both liked that rock better, now that rock was to share.

The mouse, while still little, felt BIG in his head.

And Lion? He still roared . . . but with laughter instead!

Yes, that day they BOTH learned

that, no matter your size,

We all have a mouse

AND

a lion inside.